CINDERELLA

CINDERELLA

RETOLD · BY · C · S · EVANS
AND · ILLUSTRATED · BY
ARTHUR · RACKHAM

LONDON : WILLIAM HEINEMANN

William Heinemann Ltd

15 Queen St, Mayfair, London W1X 8BE

LONDON   MELBOURNE   TORONTO
JOHANNESBURG   AUCKLAND

First published 1919
This edition 1972

Printed in Great Britain by
Colour Reproductions Limited

CINDERELLA

CHAPTER I

THE LITTLE GIRL IN THE BIG HOUSE

ONCE upon a time there was a nobleman who was married to a sweet and beautiful lady. They had one child, a little girl named Ella, and they lived in a big house in the country.

What a fine house that was ! There were more rooms in it than you could count on your fingers and toes, and each room was full of the grandest furniture. Ella had a room all to herself, with pictures of fairy-stories on the walls and cupboards full of toys, and she used to play there on wet days after she had done her lessons and her embroidery. When the weather was fine, however, Ella much preferred to play in the garden, which was so big and so full of interesting things that nobody could ever get tired of it. There was a lake in the garden with nine swans on it ; and there was a little summer-house all covered with roses ; and there was an orchard where apples and pears and plum-trees grew. At the end of a long drive, by the lodge-keeper's cottage, were the big gates that shut the garden off from the road. The road led to the town, which was a mile away, and all sorts of interesting people came walking along it—pedlar-men and beggars, and soldiers in splendid uniforms with pikes on their shoulders, marching left, right, left, right. Once Ella saw the King and Queen go by in a grand coach. The young Prince was with them, and all the people came out of their cottages to see him and to shout " Hurrah ! "—for he was a very handsome and lovable young Prince. He smiled at Ella as he went by, and she waved her hand to him, and wished he would stop and come to play with her in the garden.

Although Ella had no brothers or sisters, she seldom felt lonely, because there was always her mother to play with her and tell her stories. Her mother knew so many stories that she could tell a new one every night

almost, and they were the most interesting stories one could possibly imagine.

Now Ella's father spent most of his time in the library reading books—great heavy books without a single picture in them, and no conversations, as Ella knew well, for she had one day stolen a peep at one. Perhaps these books were full of stories ! If they were, however, her father never told her any of them. In fact, he hardly ever spoke to her or to anybody else. Every morning after breakfast he would go away to his library, and sit there reading, with a big pair of horn spectacles on his nose, or writing with a quill pen that made a funny, scratchy noise.

There were not many little girls who were happier than Ella up to the time when she was twelve years old. Then a great sorrow came into her life, for her mother was taken ill. All the cleverest doctors came from miles around to give her physic, but none of them could do any good. Ella used to stand by the window and watch them drive up in their carriages. They were most of them big, important-looking men, dressed in black, shiny silk clothes with white lace on the sleeves, and they took snuff and said " Hum—ha " a great many times. Ella was very anxious to know whether they were going to cure her dear mother, but they always spoke in very low voices, and they looked so important and so solemn that she did not dare to ask any questions.

And then one morning, when she came downstairs, she found her father sitting in the big arm-chair with his head buried in his hands. He did not say anything to

her for a long time, and then he came over and put his hand upon her head and stroked her hair.

"We are all alone now, dear," he said.

And Ella knew, without any more telling, that her mother was dead.

All that day she crept about with a white face, trying to realize what had happened to her. It seemed impossible to believe that she would never again hear her mother's voice, or see her gentle smile. At night when she went to bed she could not sleep, and at last she got up and went to the window and stood there looking into the garden. It was very dark and mysterious out there. A wind was blowing among the trees, sighing like somebody in pain, and the moon shone fitfully from behind barred clouds.

And then a strange thing happened; for as Ella stood there, with the tears which she could not restrain rolling down her cheeks, she thought she saw the figure of an old woman among the bushes on the edge of the lawn. It was too dark to see very plainly, but the strange figure seemed to be dressed in a long black cloak and a queer, pointed hat, and to be leaning on a stick. As Ella watched, the moon shone out full for a moment and lighted up the face of the woman, who was staring straight at Ella's window. It was an old face, but very, very tender, and the smile on the wrinkled lips was so beautiful that Ella stretched out her arms to the figure and gave a cry.

Then the clouds rolled over the face of the moon, and the shadows darkened in the garden; and when Ella looked again, the figure had vanished.

CHAPTER II

ELLA GOES TO SCHOOL

WHAT a change came over the house now that there was no mother to keep things in order ! Ella's father shut himself up in his library more than ever. The servants gossiped on the stairs instead of attending to their work, and Ella wandered about the house with nobody to talk to and nothing to do. Even the garden did not seem the same place, and the fruit that grew upon the south wall in the orchard seemed to have lost its flavour. There was no longer any fun in having picnics in the summer-house, for nobody swept it out nowadays, and all sorts of creepy-crawly things, such as spiders and earwigs, which Ella hated, came and made their homes there. How can you enjoy a picnic if you are always picking spiders and long-legged gnats out of your teacup ? This state of things was the fault of the gardener, who had become very lazy, and who used to spend the whole day leaning on his spade and smoking a long clay pipe.

And then a worse thing happened, for one day Ella's father told her that she must go away to school. She did not like this in the least, and begged to be allowed to stay at home and do lessons in the morning, as she had done when her mother was alive.

" All is for your own good, my dear," said her father. " There is nobody to teach you now, and you will be all the better for the society of other little girls of your own age." And so her boxes were packed and a chaise came to the door, and Ella drove away.

Ella remained at school for two whole years, and during all that time she did not see her home. Then one day her father came with the carriage to bring her back again.

When they had left the town well behind, he took Ella's little hand in his big one and said :

"You must have been very lonely in the house after your mother died. Were you not lonely, child ? "

" Yes, indeed," answered Ella, and the tears came into her eyes when she thought of the dear mother whom she would never see again in this world. " But you see," she went on, " I have been thinking over things while I have been at school, and I have made up my mind to try not to be lonely any more. There are so many things that mother used to do which I can do instead. One of these days I shall have to take her place, so I may as well begin now, mayn't I ? "

" Of course," said her father, " and you are a very good little girl to think of it ; but there has been a change while you have been away, and I want to tell you about it."

" A change ? " cried Ella, opening her eyes wide.

" Yes," the Baron went on, speaking rather fast, as though he had to say something unpleasant and wanted to get it over. " Somebody has come to live with us while you have been away—somebody who will, I hope, take a mother's place to you. A lady has—ahem—done

me the honour to accept my hand. That is to say, child,
I am married again, and my wife has two daughters who
will also live with us for the future. You must try to
like them for my sake."

This piece of news was so much of a surprise to Ella
that for a time she could not say a word. A stranger in
her mother's house, sitting in her mother's chair, doing
the things her mother used to do! The very thought
made a big lump come into her throat.

"What are their names," she said at last, "the girls'
names, I mean?"

"One is called Charlotte," answered her father, "and
the other Euphronia."

"I like the name of Charlotte," said Ella miserably.
"Are they big girls or little ones?"

"Well, you see," said her father, "correctly speaking,
they are not girls at all. That is to say, child, they have
—ahem—arrived at years of discretion. You must not
expect them to play ball or anything like that, or run
about the garden with you. They are—what shall we
say?—a little sober in temperament; but excellent
creatures, nevertheless—excellent creatures. You will
get on very well together, I'm sure, with a little give and
take on both sides."

"Just a minute, father," pleaded Ella. "Do tell me
some more about my new sisters. I cannot understand
all the big words you use. Do you mean that they are
grown up?"

Her father nodded. "In point of fact, adult," he
said, and his tone was so gloomy that Ella had to smile.

" Never mind," she said. " Some grown-ups are
very nice, especially if they know stories or can play
pretend-games, as mother used to do. Can Charlotte
and Euphronia play pretend-games, do you know ? "

" Let me see," said her father. " Charlotte plays the
spinet very nicely, I believe—her mother tells me so. I
have not heard her much myself, because I do not care
for music, and I always shut the library door when she
begins to play. Euphronia—let me see now—what is it
Euphronia does ? Oh, of course, Euphronia sings. I
gather from her mother that she is no mean performer,
though I am no judge of these things. But here we are
at the house, child, so do not ask any more questions. In
a few minutes you shall meet your stepmother and your
sisters in person."

CHAPTER III

THE HOME-COMING

HALF and hour later Ella sat alone in the middle of the big drawing-room feeling very unhappy. She had not yet seen her stepmother or her stepsisters, who were out visiting. But she had found many traces of their presence in the house.

First of all, when she had gone up to her own room she found to her dismay that somebody else had been using it. All her pictures had been taken down from the walls and replaced by ugly steel engravings. The cupboard containing her toys was nowhere to be seen, and in its place stood a tall swinging mirror. The window-seat, where she used to sit curled up on wet days reading a story-book or looking out into the garden, was not there either, nor were the pretty chintz curtains. Instead of the latter, the window was draped with an ugly red brocade, so dark and heavy that it made the entire room seem dull. Facing the window was a queerly shaped flat table with a sort of well in it, and in the well were little pots of white powder and some soft stuff that looked like cream, and sticks of red paint. There was also a small porcelain box containing little patches cut out of black plaster, which Ella knew ladies stuck on their cheeks when they were going out visiting or to a ball. Besides these, there was a hare's foot for dabbing powder on, and several powder-puffs, and half a dozen

bottles of scent and a pair of curling-tongs, and—
strangest of all—a bundle of red hair that looked like the
front part of a wig, all frizzled up into curls. The room
was very untidy, too. Skirts and other articles of clothing
were scattered about on the floor, and a hat with a big
feather in it was lying on the back of one of the chairs.
The cushions on the divan were all creased and crumpled,
and a book lay face down on the carpet just where it
had been thrown when its owner had done with it.

Ella stood and gazed at all this for some time ; then
she heard a step on the stairs, and going to the door saw
Belinda, the maid, who had come to help her unpack.

" Oh, Belinda," said Ella, " what has happened to
my room ? "

" It's not your room any longer, miss," answered
Belinda. " Miss Euphronia took such a fancy to it,
because it was pleasant and had an outlook on the
garden, that she has turned it into a dressing-room.
That's her table over there, where she titivates herself.
She has taken your bedroom, too, and put your things
up into the attic."

" I shall complain to father," said Ella. " It cannot
be his will that I should be so slighted, and he will put
matters right."

" I shouldn't count too much on that if I were you,
miss," said Belinda. " There's changes in your father,
too. He's no longer master in his own house, and he's
nagged at day and night. Why, the only peace the poor
man can get is to shut himself up in his library, and even
then the Baroness," here Belinda gave a mighty scornful

sniff, " goes and disturbs him half a dozen times a day. The poor man wouldn't even get his meals if I didn't take them up to him, for he'd rather face a den of roaring lions than the Baroness" (another sniff) " and Miss Charlotte and Miss Euphronia across the dinner-table. And small blame to him, for three more disagreeable females it's never been my ill fortune to meet. I shouldn't

count too much on your father—not if I were you, miss.
You'll just have to grin and bear it, and make the best of
things."

So it was a very miserable Ella who went upstairs to
the dark attic, which smelt of dust and spiders' webs,
and unpacked her trunk beneath the sloping roof.
Belinda had made the place look as comfortable as she

could, and had even nailed up some of the pictures on the walls ; but there was hardly room to turn round, and when Ella sat on the bed her toes almost touched the opposite wall. What a change from the pretty, airy room that had once been her own !

Her eyes were so full of tears that she could hardly see to unpack, but she wiped them away presently, and took out her prettiest dress, a white muslin, with blue embroidery on the front and a wide sash of blue silk. She put this on, because she thought she might as well look her best, and went down to the drawing-room to wait for her stepmother's return.

In a little while she heard the crunching of wheels on the drive outside, and then the banging of the front door, and the sound of high-pitched voices. It seemed as though a quarrel were going on, for the voices were very loud and very bad-tempered.

" I tell you, he bowed to *me*."

" Stuff and nonsense ! I'll warrant he never even noticed you. He looked straight at me as he walked by the carriage, and I smiled in return."

" Forward creature !—when you had never been introduced."

" Minx ! "

" Cat ! "

And so the two went on, snapping and snarling, until a deeper voice put in, " For goodness' sake stop your bickering, you two ; do now, and help me off with this turban. I don't expect he bowed to either of you ; and if he did, it doesn't matter, for he's nothing but a country squire's son with not a penny in his pocket. I wonder whether that brat of the Baron's has come home ? "

"That's my stepmother," thought Ella, " and the Baron's brat is me ! Oh dear. I wish I'd stayed at school ! " She had half a thought of escaping through the French windows into the garden and running away ; but before she could move a step the drawing-room door flew open, and in came the Baroness with her two daughters.

CHAPTER IV

THE BARONESS AND HER DAUGHTERS

HAVE you ever noticed that there are some people whom you know you are not going to like the first time you set eyes on them? Well, the Baroness was one of those people, and so were the two

sisters—for three more disagreeable-looking persons never
walked into a room together.

The Baroness came first, striding along in a proud
and haughty manner, and peering through a pair of
tortoise-shell-rimmed spectacles which she carried at the
end of a long handle. She was fat and stumpy, with
more than one chin, and she had cross, crafty eyes set
very close together over a big hooked nose. The fingers
of her hands were covered with flashing rings, among

which, to her horror, Ella recognized one that had belonged to her mother, and she was dressed in a gown of black and yellow like a gipsy at a fair.

Ella rose and dropped a curtsy as her father introduced her, while the Baroness stared at her from head to toe through her lorgnette.

"So this is the girl," she said at last in a harsh voice. "How do you do, miss? I've heard of your airs and graces, and the way you have been mollycoddled, and I want you to understand that that sort of thing has come to an end now. You've been to school, I believe."

"Yes," faltered Ella.

"Don't they teach you to say madam when you speak to your elders? Who told you to put on that frock?"

"Nobody," said Ella, whose face was red with shame. "It is my frock which my father gave to me, and I put it on because I like it best of all my frocks."

"Oh, indeed! Then you may go and take it off as quickly as you like, and put on the plainest one you have. I don't like little girls who give themselves airs. Why do you not greet your sisters?"

Now this was hardly fair, for poor little Ella had not had time to greet anybody, or to do anything except answer questions, since her new relations had arrived. Nevertheless, she tried to smile and to appear friendly. "How do you do?" she said. "My father told me about you as we were coming home in the carriage. I think you've got such pretty names! But I don't know yet which is Charlotte and which is Euphronia, so I can't call you by them!"

"Do you hear that, mamma?" cried one of the girls. "She actually came home in one of our carriages! I suppose she considers herself too much of a fine lady to walk."

The one who spoke was red-haired, and her face was highly rouged and powdered, so Ella judged that it was she who had taken possession of her room. But in spite of her paint and powder nobody could possibly call this girl handsome. To begin with, she squinted so badly that while one eye was looking at Ella, the gaze of the other was fixed on the corner of the room. And, as if this was not enough, she had inherited her mother's big hooked nose, which made her face look rather like that of a horse, although no horse could possibly have worn so bad-tempered and discontented an expression.

The other sister, who, as Ella afterwards learned, was the one named Charlotte, was no beauty either, but she was considerably more attractive than Euphronia, though she had a little red nose that was turned up in the most comical way. Nevertheless, Ella thought that there was just a trace of kindliness in Charlotte's look, so she ventured to appeal to her.

"I am sorry if I did wrong by coming home in the carriage," she said, "but my father came to the school for me. Please do not be angry, and I will try to please you in future."

"Come, come," said the Baron, nervously rubbing his hands. "Do not let us begin to quarrel about such a little thing. The child is really not at fault."

" Hold your tongue, Charles," snapped his wife. " And please understand that I will not have the creature pampered. We shall have her demanding a boudoir next, and a servant to wait on her ! "

" But, my dear . . ." stammered the Baron.

" Don't talk to me," cried his wife, with an angry stamp of the foot. " We shall see whether or not I am to be mistress in my own house ! Euphronia, take this naughty girl up into the garret, and lock her in until she comes to her senses. A few days of solitude and a diet of bread and water will do her all the good in the world."

" Come along, you stuck-up little thing," said Euphronia, seizing Ella's wrist with her large bony hand. " You will have to be taught your proper place."

And so Ella was dragged away. At the door she turned an appealing glance towards her father, but he was looking at his toes and made no movement to interfere.

The last thing Ella heard as she went up the stairs was the voice of the Baroness storming at her husband. Even when the door of the garret was slammed upon her she could still hear it, deep and booming, like the rumble of distant thunder !

CHAPTER V

HOW ELLA BECAME CINDERELLA

SO there was poor little Ella in the dark garret at the top of the house, where she remained for twenty-four hours with no food but bread and water. There was nothing in the room except a straw mattress which had been turned out of one of the servants' chambers, and on this she lay down, burying her head in her hands, and sobbing as if her heart would break. What hurt her more than anything else was the thought that her father had done nothing to protect her against her stepmother's ill-treatment. She had wild thoughts of running away and going to the town to hire herself as a maid-of-all-work at one of the inns, but the little window of her room was barred on the outside, so she had perforce to stay where she was until it pleased her captors to come and let her out.

Presently it grew dark, and then the loneliness was awful ; but Ella shut her eyes and consoled herself by thinking about the happy days she used to spend when her mother was alive. After a time she fell into a sleep, and in her dreams it seemed to her as though her mother was standing beside the wretched bed, looking down upon her with eyes of pity and of love.

It was Euphronia who came the next day to let Ella out. She threw open the door and stood on the threshold for a time, smiling spitefully.

" Well, miss," she said, " and how did you like your bedroom ? Did you find it airy and comfortable ? "

" Why are you so horrid to me ? " asked Ella. " I'm sure I've done nothing to deserve it. If you do not like to have me in the house I will go away and not trouble you any more. Let me go back to school and spend my holidays there, as I have done before."

" A splendid idea," mocked Euphronia, " and I've no doubt it is just what you would like. There is to be no more school for you, miss. Too much money has been wasted on you already, and we will certainly spend no more. What does a little chit like you want of learning Italian and history and dancing ! You will have to make yourself useful now, and do something to earn your keep ! "

If anybody had told Ella a day or two before that she would have been miserable at the idea of not being allowed to go back to school, she would not have believed them ; but at these words her heart sank. What further humiliations had Fate in store ?

She was soon to learn, for Euphronia hustled her off into the kitchen and made her sit down at the table with the servants. There she was given a hunk of coarse bread and a mugful of milk, and told to eat heartily because that was all she would get until the following morning. She learnt, too, that she was not even to have the attic where she had unpacked her clothes, but was to sleep henceforward in the very garret where she had been imprisoned, on that ragged straw mattress that had not been good enough for a scullion.

" Oh, Belinda," sobbed Ella, when her sister at last had gone away. " I am the most unhappy girl in all the world. Whatever shall I do ? "

" Put a bold face on it, missy," said Belinda, " and keep up your courage. Perhaps they don't mean all they say, and will be kinder to you when they have worked off their spite. At any rate, nothing is to be gained by crying your pretty eyes out."

" You will be good to me, won't you, Belinda, and let me stay here ? I never want to go upstairs again while my stepmother and my stepsisters are in the house. We can be quite cosy together, and I'll help you all I can, and teach you some of the things I have learnt at school."

" That would be very nice, missy," answered Belinda, " and you may stay here and welcome, but I'm afraid you won't have my company, because I'm leaving at the end of the week. All the house servants are under notice to leave. The mistress says she means to economize and to stop the waste that has been going on for years. I expect she wants the money to buy jewels to hang on herself and her ugly daughters. Ugh, the nasty creatures ! " And Belinda shook her head and walked away muttering.

Ella was very dejected at the prospect of losing one whom she had come to consider her only friend in the world ; but before a week had gone by she discovered that Belinda's words were only too true. One by one the servants left, until there was nobody left in the kitchen but Ella herself and a little scullery-maid who sniffed all day long through her nose and walked about on shoes that had no heels.

Now Ella discovered what her stepsister had meant when she said that she had got to learn to make herself useful. For a day or two she was left to do as she liked, and then one morning Euphronia came down to the kitchen and found her sitting at the window reading a book.

" Well I never ! " cried Euphronia. " So that's how you spend your time ! Come here at once, and put on this coarse apron and then go down on your knees and scrub the floor."

" I am doing no harm," said Ella mildly. " Mother always used to let me read in the morning, after my lessons were done. As for the floor, it is quite clean, for the scullery-maid has only just finished scrubbing it. Please, Euphronia, let me go on with my work."

" What, what ! " screamed Euphronia, working herself up into a fine rage. " More airs and graces ! Take that, you miserable brat, and that, for daring to be impudent to your betters ! " And with her great hard hand she struck poor Ella several blows on the cheek. Then the poor girl was locked up in the garret once more and almost starved until her spirit was broken.

Things went on in this way for over a month, during which Ella never saw her father or her stepmother. Euphronia was her taskmistress, and she seemed to take a delight in heaping insults and cruelties upon Ella's head. Sometimes Charlotte came down into the kitchen and stood watching while Ella cleaned the silver, or did some similar menial work, but she did not say anything, except to quarrel with her elder sister, in which occupation these two amiable beings seemed to pass the greater part of their time.

Little by little Ella became accustomed to her new position, and took up more and more of the duties of a kitchen-maid. Early in the morning she would rise from her bed and go downstairs to rake out the grates and light the fires. Then she would wash up the greasy crockery left over from the previous night's dinner, and sweep the kitchen floor, and prepare a dish of tea to take up to her stepsisters, who always lay abed until ten or eleven o'clock in the morning. Euphronia looked so funny in bed with her false curls off and her bald forehead showing that Ella felt very much inclined to laugh, but she dared not for fear of a beating. Both the sisters were lazybones, and even when they did arouse themselves to get up, they would walk about the house in their wrappers, with untidy, down-at-heel slippers on their feet. Ella grew to hate the sound of their footsteps —slip-slop, slip-slop, over the polished floors.

When her frugal breakfast was done Ella began the work of the day. Sometimes it was the stairs that had to be brushed down, or the bedrooms to be turned out, or the drawing-room to be cleaned. All the bedrooms had parquet floors, which Ella had to polish on her hands and knees until she could see her face in them. Very hard work it was, and her delicate little hands, which had once been so soft and white, grew coarse and hard.

From morning till night she was kept busy, with hardly a moment to rest except at meal-times. Only after dinner in the evening had she an hour or two to herself, and then she used to go and sit in the big open fireplace on a low stool close to the smouldering wood cinders, and, with her head resting on her hands, think of her hard lot, and of the happy days that were gone by.

During the first six months she had no companion except the little scullery-maid, who always seemed to have a cold in her nose, and who was not very good company at the best of times. When this maid left, Ella was allowed to go into the drawing-room now and then to read to the sisters, or to do a bit of embroidery.

" I hope, child," said Mistress Euphronia on one of these occasions, " that you realize how fortunate you are in being allowed to improve your mind by reading books and by listening to good music ! " (By good music she meant her singing to Charlotte's accompaniment on the harpsichord. She made the most dreadful noises.) " But I'll warrant," she went on, " that you are much happier downstairs with your pots and pans, or sitting among the cinders. Come, confess now, are you not happier so ? "

" Yes," said Ella quietly.

For some reason this reply seemed to make Euphronia very angry, and the next night, when Ella went up into the drawing-room, she said with a spiteful smile, " I have found a new name for you. In future I shall call you Cinderslut because of your nasty habit of sitting

among the cinders. Come, Cinderslut, and hold this
skein of wool for me."

At this Ella flushed and was about to make an angry reply, when Charlotte, who was never quite so unkind to her as the other, said, " No, no, sister, let us call her Cinder-Ella, that sounds much better."

And Cinderella it was from that time forward.

CHAPTER VI

THE INVITATION

THINGS went on in this way for more than two years, and during all that time Cinderella seldom spoke to her father. There was no doubt that he knew how his little daughter was being treated, but he gave no sign that he knew, or that he tried to prevent it. The fact is, he was so much afraid of his new wife that he dared not say a word. He shut himself up in his library more and more, and Cinderella heard from her step-sisters that he was engaged in writing a book.

" It's all about the Greeks," said Euphronia, " nasty unfashionable creatures who lived in tubs and went about with lanterns looking for honest people." I think she was thinking of the story of Diogenes, which Cinderella had told her one day when the name came up in the course of her reading from a news-sheet; but can you understand such ignorance !

Once the Baron came out of his room while Cinderella was brushing the stairs. He put his hand on her head as he used to do in the old days, and looked as if he were going to say something, but the sound of his wife's footsteps on the stairs startled him, and he scuttled back to his room like a frightened rabbit.

Cinderella was now sixteen years of age, and in spite of her hard life had grown to be a very beautiful girl. Her pretty clothes had long ago worn out, or become too

small for her, and she had to dress in odds and ends
which were left off by her sisters. This would not have
mattered very much if the clothes had been in good taste,
for it is quite possible to look well even if one's clothes
are shabby, but both the sisters had a liking for violent
colours and tasteless finery. Thus, for instance, Euphronia would come down in the evening in a gown of
yellow covered with black stripes, which made her look
like a zebra. You can imagine the effect of it, in contrast
with her red hair and painted cheeks. Charlotte, on
the other hand, loved purple and green, and she would
produce the most astonishing effects by mixing these

two colours. Nothing was ever given to Cinderella until it was almost in rags, and she had the greatest difficulty in keeping herself respectable. In spite of her ragged clothes, however, she always managed to look a thousand times more beautiful than the sisters.

And now we come to the turning-point of Cinderella's life. You remember the handsome young Prince, whom

Ella had once seen driving with the King and Queen along the road that ran past the house. He had now reached the age of twenty-one years, and on the occasion of his birthday there were to be great festivities. Cinderella heard all about it from her sisters. For weeks beforehand they had talked of nothing else in the evenings when Cinderella went into the drawing-room. They even neglected their music, and were so excited that they stopped in the middle of a most fascinating novel they were reading. The novel was about a poor but noble young man who was dispossessed of his rightful inheritance by a wicked uncle, and it always made Euphronia cry.

" They say that the whole town is to be illuminated," said Charlotte, " and the fountains are going to run with wine, so that the common people can enjoy themselves."

" I don't see why the common people need to enjoy themselves," said Euphronia with a sniff. " The Prince would do much better to devote his attention to the fashionable folk and the gentry. What do a lot of greasy peasants and shopkeepers want with illuminations and fountains running wine ? "

" Every boy-child in the town is to have a present," Charlotte went on, " and every girl-child a doll. That is by the Prince's own wish, for he is very fond of children."

" Sentimental nonsense ! " cried Euphronia, tossing her head.

" And there are to be a series of grand balls at the palace, to which all the best people in the country are to be invited. We shall get an invitation, of course, for we are very important people."

" Yes," replied Euphronia, " we shall certainly receive an invitation," and she was right. For one afternoon a courier from the palace came riding to the house and delivered the invitation in a large envelope, sealed with the royal seal.

Now what a scene of excitement there was ! The sisters spent half the day talking about what they were going to wear, and the other half grimacing before their looking-glasses. All the dresses were brought out of the wardrobe, and Cinderella was called upstairs to admire them and to give her advice.

" I think I shall wear my red velvet gown with the English point-lace trimmings," said Euphronia. " That is so dignified and stately, and it suits me admirably."

" As for me," said Charlotte, " I shall put on my purple petticoat and my green cloak that is brocaded in gold. Purple, you know, is the royal colour, and it is therefore most appropriate for a royal ball."

Then they put the dresses on, and stalked about the room in them, posturing before the mirrors and practising graceful bows and curtsies. At all hours of the day errand-boys came from the shops in the town carrying parcels—new shawls and lace kerchiefs and fancy shoes, bottles containing toilet-water and scent, boxes of black patches from the best makers and of the latest shape, fans and gloves and jewelled clasps—one would have thought that there were fifty people in the house who were going to the ball instead of only two. Cinderella was kept busy from morning till night, ironing the sisters' linen and goffering their ruffles.

When the great day arrived, Cinderella was called upstairs to help the sisters dress. The ball did not begin until seven o'clock in the evening, but they began their preparations immediately after breakfast, and even rose at eight o'clock, which was a thing they had never done before in all their lives.

Cinderella found their room in the most hopeless confusion. There were hats and feathers on the bed, skirts and petticoats of different colours strewed all over

the floor, pins and curling-tongs and bottles on the
toilet-table, and jewel-cases on the chairs. Euphronia
was sitting before the mirror trying to arrange her hair
over a great frame that rose a foot above her forehead ;
and as there was so little of it, she was having considerable
difficulty. She was already dressed in her red velvet
gown with green stockings and gold shoes, and she
looked rather like a very large and brilliantly coloured
cockatoo.

On the other side of the room, Charlotte was engaged in lacing her bodice, and had already broken a dozen laces in the attempt to make her waist smaller than nature ever intended it to be.

"Come here, you lazy little thing," screamed Euphronia as soon as Cinderella entered the room; "come and hold these pins for me while I dress my hair. A plague on the hairdresser who sent me this cream, for it won't keep a curl in its place. I'm driven nearly distracted."

"Would you like me to dress your hair for you?" asked Cinderella. "I'm sure I could do it if you would let me try!"

"No, no," cried Charlotte. "I want Cinderella to come and pull these laces a little tighter. This bodice will close quite another inch with careful coaxing."

"Oh, you abominably selfish creature! You know very well that all the tugging in the world will not make you look genteel. It is only wasting time, and my hair must be done or I shall be late for the ball."

And so they began one of their quarrels, and Cinderella had to soothe them by offering to do Euphronia's hair first and to lace Charlotte afterwards. Beneath her deft fingers the unruly tresses soon fell into shape, and Euphronia, watching the happy result of her work in the mirror, grew quite gracious.

"That's very becoming," she said, stretching her lean neck this way and that. "Auburn hair is quite the fashion this year, according to the *Court Intelligencer*. I'm positive that I shall create a great sensation. Don't

you wish that you were going to the ball with us,
Cinderella ? "

" Why do you make fun of me ? " said Cinderella
sadly ; " you know very well that such things are not
for me."

" You are right ! " cried Euphronia with a spiteful
laugh. " Fancy a Cinderslut at the Prince's ball ! How
everybody would laugh ! "

Cinderella felt very much inclined to give her stepsister's hair a tug, or at the very least to dress it awry ;
but she controlled herself with an effort, and went on
quietly with her task.

" They say," remarked Charlotte, who was carefully
fixing a patch shaped like a coach and four on her cheek
—" they say that the Prince is to choose a bride from
among the high-born ladies who will be present at the
ball. Oh, sister, suppose it should be me ! "

" Pooh ! What nonsense ! " replied Euphronia with
a giggle. " How do you get such fancies in your head ?
The Prince would be just as likely to choose Cinderslut
here. Besides, he has dark hair and eyes, and it is well
known that dark people always prefer women who are
blonde, and have a touch of colour in their com-
plexion."

And in another minute they were at it again, quarrel-
ling hammer and tongs, so that Cinderella's head nearly
burst with the din. At last, however, everything was
ready, the carriage came to the door, and they drove
away, leaving poor Cinderella gazing sadly out of the
window after them.

CHAPTER VII

THE FAIRY GODMOTHER

CINDERELLA followed the carriage with her eyes until it was out of sight, and then she descended to the kitchen, and took up her usual place in the corner of the fireplace.

She felt very miserable as she sat there in the chimney corner. She was of a brave disposition, and she had learned not to show her feelings in the presence of her stepsisters, but as she contrasted their good fortune with her hard and miserable life she could not help crying. By this time they were in the great hall of the palace, mingling with a crowd of gaily dressed and happy people, beneath the light of a thousand candles,

while she sat there in the dingy kitchen, with no one to
talk to, and only her sad thoughts for occupation. A
tear fell down her nose and splashed on to the hearth-
stone, and then another and another.

All of a sudden Cinderella heard a noise. She nearly
jumped out of her skin when she saw the figure of an
old woman standing in the shadow on the other side of
the hearth-place.

" Who are you ? " asked Cinderella in a quavering
voice.

" Don't be afraid," said the woman. " I have not
come to do you any harm. You have seen me before,
once upon a time, when you were even more unhappy
than you are to-night. Look at me well, and see if you
do not remember."

Then the strange old woman stepped forward into the
light. She was very, very old ; so old that her face was
a maze of lines, like a wrinkled apple. She was dressed
in a very full red petticoat and a black-laced bodice, and

on her head was a queerly shaped hat, with a high pointed crown and a wide brim. There she stood, leaning heavily on a big crooked stick, while Cinderella gazed at her and wondered where she had seen her before.

And then the woman smiled.

Have you ever seen a ray of sunshine light up the shadows of a gloomy place? Well, the strange woman's smile was like that. She no longer appeared old, but as young and radiant as a spring morning, and her eyes glowed deep and pure and true.

" I know, I know ! " cried Cinderella. " You are the woman who was in the garden that night when my mother died. The moon pointed you out to me, and I wanted to come down to you, but when I looked again you had disappeared."

" Because the time was not ripe," said the woman. " You only saw me that once, but many is the time that I have seen you. I have watched you at your work day after day, and I know all that you have endured through the malice of your stepmother and your stepsisters. At night, when you sat here brooding among the cinders and thought yourself all alone, I was never very far away. When you went to your garret and lay down on your straw bed, it was I who watched over your sleep."

" Why," said Cinderella, " who then can you be ? "

" I am your godmother," answered the old woman. " Your mother and I were friends when she was a girl, and I promised her before she died that I would make your welfare my care. You were crying when I came in. Tell me what was the matter ? "

"It was nothing," said Cinderella, who was just a little ashamed at having been discovered in tears. "I wanted—I wanted——"

"You wanted to go to the ball—isn't that it?"

"Yes," said Cinderella with a sigh.

"Well, if you will be a good girl and do what I tell you, and don't ask any questions, you shall go. Have you a pumpkin-bed in the garden?"

"Why, yes," said Cinderella wonderingly.

"Then go to it at once, and bring me the biggest pumpkin you can find. Now don't stop to ask me why, but just do as I say, and you will discover the reason quickly enough."

Cinderella ran into the garden at once, and soon came back with a fine pumpkin, which she gave to her godmother, wondering the while how such a thing was going to help her to go to the ball.

"Now a knife, if you please."

Cinderella brought a knife, with which her godmother cut off the top of the pumpkin and scooped out the pulp until nothing was left but the hollow rind.

This she took outside into the courtyard and touched with her stick, when the pumpkin immediately changed into a most magnificent coach, all glass above and gilded panels below!

Now Cinderella realized that her godmother was a fairy, and if there was a more surprised and delighted girl in the whole country that night, I have yet to hear of her. She could not resist peeping inside the coach, which was upholstered with delicate rose-coloured silk, and she was so excited that her godmother had to touch her on the arm to bring her to herself.

" Come along," said the old woman, " or the ball will be over before you get there. I want a mouse or two. Run and see if there are any in the trap."

Cinderella hastened into the kitchen and found that, by the greatest good luck, there were six live mice in the trap. There they were, running round and round the wire cage, and poking their little black muzzles through the bars.

" Open the trap just a little," said the old woman, " and let them run out one by one." Then, as each mouse came out, she gave it a tap with her stick, and each mouse was immediately changed into a fine horse. When she had finished there was a train of handsome steeds, all of a dappled mouse-grey colour, and so well trained that they immediately placed themselves between the shafts of the carriage, ready to be harnessed into place.

" Now we shall want a coachman," said the old woman when this was done. " What are we going to do for him, I wonder ? "

" I know," said Cinderella. " Perhaps there is a rat in the rat-trap. If so, he'll make a very good coachman. I'll go and see."

Once again fortune favoured her. There were no less than three large rats in the rat-trap, and that was a very unusual thing.

" A very fine selection," said the fairy godmother

looking them over. " We'll have this fat fellow, because
he has such a splendid set of whiskers. Let him out
carefully."

She touched the rat with her wand, and before
Cinderella's eyes he grew taller and taller and gradually
changed shape.

First of all his hind legs became a pair of shapely legs, clad in a pair of most elegant grey breeches : then his tail shrivelled up and turned into the tail of a fine, grey livery-coat. The last part of him to change was his head, so that the rat could watch the strange things that were happening to his person.

You never saw a more surprised-looking rat in your life ! However, there he stood at last, the most dignified and solemn-looking coachman that ever sat on a box-seat, and his whiskers were a real wonder to behold.

" With such a fine coach and six you must have some footmen," the godmother said. " Go into the garden

again and look behind the big watering-pot that stands
beside the fountain. There you will find six lizards.
Catch them and bring them to me, but mind you don't
catch hold of their tails, because if you do the tails will
come off in your hand, and in that case your footmen
will have no coats to their backs."

58 The lizards were behind the watering-pot, just as the old woman had said, and fine plump fellows they were. Very soon they were turned into six footmen, all as like each other as six peas in a pod, and all dressed in a showy livery of grey and gold. They did not need to

be taught their duties, but jumped up behind the coach
and held on to the rail there, just as if they had done
nothing else all their lives.

"So that is finished," said the fairy godmother with
a smile. "There is no lady at the Prince's ball to-night

who will arrive in a finer equipage than you. Are you not pleased ? "

" Yes," answered Cinderella, " but am I to go to the ball in these shabby old clothes ? Everybody would stare at me ! "

" Bless my soul, I forgot all about the dress ! " cried the old woman ; " but that is easily attended to." She touched Cinderella lightly on the shoulder with her stick, and immediately her dingy gown was changed into a magnificent dress of white silk, embroidered with butterflies and flowers of a delicate blue, and sewn with seed-pearls. Round her neck was a necklace of pearls and diamonds, and, greatest wonder of all, on her tiny feet was a pair of glass shoes, the prettiest that ever were seen.

" Now you are all ready," said the kind godmother who had worked all these marvels. " Step into the coach and drive away, but before you go, take careful heed of what I say. You may dance and enjoy yourself to your heart's content until midnight, but on the stroke of twelve you must leave the ballroom and come home. If you remain even a minute longer, your coach will become a pumpkin, your horses mice, your coachman a rat, and your footmen lizards, while your pretty gown will change back again into your shabby old dress. That will not be nice for you, to have such things happening in everybody's sight, so remember my warning."

Cinderella promised her godmother that she would not fail to act upon her advice, and, stepping into her coach, drove off, almost beside herself with joy.

CHAPTER VIII

THE BALL

AWAY went the grand coach, down the drive and through the lodge gates (which were standing wide open), and out on to the wide road that led to the town. The six grey horses stepped as proudly as any steeds in the King's own stable ; the coachman sat on the box as dignified as an emperor, and all the six footmen clung on behind and called out " Make way ! Make way ! " Through the town they clattered, to the amazement and joy of all the folk who were making holiday. The housewives came to their windows to see, and the citizens waved their caps in the air and shouted out " Hurrah ! " They thought that Cinderella was a princess, or a duchess at least.

That, too, was the opinion of the ushers when the carriage drew up before the palace gates. The ushers came out to ask the name of the new guest, but Cinderella told her footmen to say that she wished her name to be kept secret. At this the ushers were puzzled and did not know what to do, so they brought the Court Chamberlain, who came out with his gold stick of office in his hand, but had to retire no wiser than he came. In his turn the Chamberlain informed the young Prince, whose curiosity was so strongly aroused that he descended in person to see who his mysterious guest could be. As soon as he saw Cinderella he was so overcome by her

beauty that he forgot all else, and, handing her down
from the carriage, escorted her into the ballroom on his
arm.

And now what a sight met Cinderella's eyes ! Many
a time since the invitation to the ball had come, she had
tried to picture the splendours of the scene, but the
reality was even more wonderful than her dreams.

The great hall was lighted by a thousand candles set
in chandeliers of cut glass that shimmered and sparkled
with all the hues of the rainbow. The room was so big
that one could hardly see the end of it, and the floor was

polished to such a degree that it reflected the light of the candles and the gay colours of the dancers' costumes. All the guests were assembled ; the fiddlers were playing merrily, and the King and Queen themselves had stepped out to lead the dance.

The entrance of Cinderella on the Prince's arm made a great sensation. Everybody stopped dancing to look at her, and even the fiddlers, amazed at her beauty, forgot to play, and sat gaping in surprise. The King, old as he was, could not take his eyes off her, and was heard to say to the Queen that it was a long time since he had seen anybody so lovely.

"Will you not tell me your name, sweet lady ? " whispered the Prince as he led her forward to present her to his father and mother.

But Cinderella shook her head and told him that she was under a vow, so the Prince, who was very polite and

amiable, was content, and did not ask her again. He thought that she was certainly a lady of very high rank, not only because of the magnificence of her carriage and the richness of her costume, but also because she was so beautiful and well-mannered. Anybody could see she was nobly born.

So she was presented to the King and Queen by a name which the Prince made up for the occasion, and they were delighted with her, and spoke to her very graciously. Then the music began again, and the Prince bowed before her and asked her if he might have the honour of a dance.

Now what would have happened to Cinderella if she had not profited by her dancing lessons at school? One never knows how soon the time may come when one will be glad of one's accomplishments. As it was, there was no lady in the hall who could dance more gracefully than she. Her little feet, clad in their shimmering glass slippers, tripped the measure as lightly as though they were treading on air. It was a joy to see her.

Meanwhile, all the guests were asking each other questions.

" Oh, how lovely she is ! " said one. " Who can she be ? "

" She must be some princess from foreign parts," said another, " for she certainly does not belong to any of the families of the province."

" Send a lackey down to the courtyard," said another, " and let him look at the coat of arms on her carriage-panels. That will tell us what we want to know."

This was done ; but the carriage-panels were not ornamented with any device, so the inquisitive guests were no wiser.

Still others followed Cinderella with their eyes and took careful note of her costume. " Whoever can her dressmaker be ? " they said. " Did you ever see such wonderful fit and style. I must certainly copy that dress for my next ball, although I am afraid the material must be very costly."

And so they continued to chatter to one another, while Cinderella, though she could not help hearing some of

their remarks, carried herself so simply and modestly
that all hearts went out to her. Almost as soon as she
had entered the ballroom she had caught a glimpse of
her stepsisters craning their necks to gaze at her from
behind the last row of the guests, and now she saw them
again, sitting rather disconsolately against the wall, for
nobody wanted to dance with such disagreeable-looking
creatures.

Dance succeeded dance, and the Prince never once left Cinderella's side. He seemed to have no eyes for anybody else, and quite neglected his other guests. Half-way through the evening, Cinderella said to him :

" Tell me, Prince, who are those two ladies sitting over there in the alcove by the pillar ? Poor things, they have not been asked to dance once the whole evening. I feel quite sorry for them."

The Prince gave a careless glance at Charlotte and Euphronia, who, indeed, looked very sour and miserable. " I do not know their names," said he, " but they are probably the daughters of one of the neighbouring squires. If you like, I will send the Master of the Ceremonies to find them partners."

" Do so, if you please," said Cinderella, " for I am sure that they are not enjoying themselves at all—and that is a pity when everybody should be so happy ! "

" You are as good and as kind-hearted as you are beautiful," said the Prince as he went away to give the necessary orders ; but he did not say it aloud, though he was longing to tell Cinderella how much he admired her.

In this way the two stepsisters found partners at last, and they never knew that it was to Cinderella that they owed their good fortune. Their plain faces glowed with pleasure when two noble gentlemen led them out to dance the cotillion, and though, if truth be told, they danced it very badly, they were quite unaware of it, for their partners were far too polite to show any annoyance at their clumsiness.

Presently a magnificent supper was served in the banqueting-hall of the palace.

That was a wonderful feast! Cinderella had never seen the like of it in all her life. The table was loaded with the rarest and costliest dishes. There were great boars' heads, swimming in gravy, on silver platters, with their eyes and tusks shining like life, and lemons in their mouths. There were great joints of beef and venison, each large enough to feed a family, and pies out of which live birds flew when the crust was opened, just like the pie in the nursery rhyme. There were cakes all covered with icing and shaped like castles or ships, and stands heaped high with the most delicious fruits.

Cinderella managed to seat herself opposite her sisters. They had not the slightest idea who she was, for they had only seen her dressed in rags, or odds and ends, with the marks of her menial toil about her. If anybody had told them that this lovely lady, the belle of the ball, was the despised Cinderslut from their own kitchen, they would never have believed it.

Cinderella went out of her way to be amiable with her sisters, and they were very proud of the attention she paid them. Many a girl, remembering their spiteful ways, would have taken advantage of her position to get her revenge, but not so Cinderella, who was good-natured and bore no malice.

" Will you not have some of these delicious citrons ? " she said, when one of the servants brought her the fruit in a silver basket. And whenever any special delicacy was brought to her, she insisted upon sharing it with them.

After the banquet, dancing began again, and the Prince, who had hardly eaten a morsel, so absorbed was he in gazing at Cinderella's beauty, renewed his attentions

to her.   Cinderella was so happy that the hours passed
by like minutes, and almost before she knew it the night
slipped away.   Suddenly, however, she heard the great
clock in the tower chime out three-quarters past eleven,
and she remembered her godmother's warning.

She rose immediately, and making a deep curtsy of
farewell, told the Prince that the time had come for her
to depart.   He pressed her to stay another hour, another
five minutes even, but she would not, and, hastening
down the stairs, jumped into the coach which was
already waiting for her, and gave the word to drive
away.   The horses galloped like the wind, and reached
the house only just in time, for just as she was entering
the clock struck twelve.

Immediately the coach vanished, and nothing was to
be seen but the hollow rind of a pumpkin lying on the
flagstones ; the coachman with the whiskers turned into
a rat again, the horses became mice, and the footmen
lizards.   The little creatures scampered away in all direc-
tions until not a tail of them was to be seen, and Cinderella stood there at the kitchen door once again attired
in her ragged clothes.

CHAPTER IX

THE SECOND NIGHT

CINDERELLA went into the kitchen where her godmother was waiting for her.

"So there you are," said the old woman. "I was just getting anxious about you. I thought you might have been tempted to disregard my warning, which would have been a great disaster. Did you enjoy yourself at the ball?"

"Oh, godmother," cried Cinderella, her eyes sparkling, "it was lovely, and I would have liked to stay there for ever. The Prince was so kind to me and paid me such honour that one would have thought I was the greatest lady in the land. There is to be another ball to-morrow night, and the Prince has invited me. I should so much like to go."

"Well, we will see about that," said her godmother. "But be very careful what you say to your stepsisters. Do not let your excitement run away with you, or you will spoil everything."

Just then there came a loud knocking at the door. It was the sisters returning. The old woman stepped back and vanished up the chimney, and Cinderella ran to let the sisters in.

"Heigho!" she said, rubbing her eyes and yawning as though she had just awakened from sleep. "How late you are! You must be tired out."

"Tired, do you say?" cried Euphronia. "If you had been to the ball, child, I'll warrant you would be less sleepy than you are. But there," she continued with a scornful sniff, "what can one expect a kitchen-wench to know of the doings of high life!"

"I suppose it was very wonderful!" said Cinderella humbly.

"Yes, indeed," said Charlotte. "There came to the ball the most beautiful Princess that ever was seen, and she paid us great attentions, I can tell you. She talked to us for the greater part of the evening, and even sat opposite to us at supper and gave us oranges and citrons."

"Do tell me about her," said Cinderella, in great delight. "What was her name, and how was she dressed?"

"That is the strange part of it," said Charlotte. "Nobody knew who she was or whence she came, though it was plain to see that she was a very grand Princess. The King's son was very puzzled about it, and we heard him say, after she had gone, that he would give all he had in the world to know her name. As for her dress, I cannot even begin to describe it. It was just a little bit too plain and lacking in colour for my taste, but the material was certainly most costly, and the fashion highly original!"

"Oh dear!" sighed Cinderella. "I do wish that I could see her! Will you not let me go with you to-morrow night? I could wear that yellow dress of Euphronia's if she would lend it to me."

"What!" screamed Euphronia. "I never heard

such impudence in my life ! Lend you my yellow dress, indeed—I like that ! Besides, it would be an insult to such a grand company to have a wretched Cinderslut among them at the ball. The Princess would never speak to us again."

Cinderella made no reply—and, to tell the truth, she was delighted by Euphronia's refusal to lend her the gown. If she had it, she would not have known what to do with it.

The next day the sisters slept very late, and even Cinderella did not rise till past her usual hour. When breakfast was over, another scene of excitement began, for the sisters had to dress themselves for the second ball, and both of them wanted their dresses altered as

much in the style of the strange Princess's gown as
possible. Cinderella, of course, knew better than either
of them what that style was, but nothing she could do
was right, and she was very glad when at last the time
came for them to go and she was alone in the house.

It was a quarter to seven, and as yet there was no
sign of her godmother. Anxiously Cinderella watched
the clock, the hands of which had never seemed to move
so slowly before, and she was just beginning to despair
of the old woman's coming when she heard a cough
behind her, and, turning quickly, saw her standing in the
doorway.

" Ha-ha ! " said the old woman, smiling. " You were
getting impatient, I see ! Well, well, I will not chide

you. Have you got the pumpkin-rind and the mouse-trap and all the rest of the things ? "

"Yes, yes, here they are," cried Cinderella, "all except the lizards, and I will go and fetch them at once. There are six more mice in the trap, and a rat that will make the most magnificent coachman. Oh, godmother, how good you are to me!"

She danced with joy as the old woman, with a touch of her stick, caused the grand coach and horses, the portly coachman and the lackeys to appear. Last of all, she received a touch on the shoulder herself, and her rags gave place to a dress that was even more magnificent than the one she had worn on the previous night. This time it was of the palest yellow silk, shaded in colour like a tea-rose, and the glass shoes on her feet were delicately edged with gold.

Once again the old woman warned her not on any account to stay at the palace after twelve o'clock, for on the last stroke of the hour all her beautiful things would change back again, and she would appear as a mere kitchen-maid, garbed in rags. Cinderella promised to give heed to her words and drove away.

When she arrived at the palace she found the Prince already waiting for her, all on fire with impatience, for he had begun to fear that she was not coming. As before, he led her into the ballroom on his arm, and gave her the place of honour among his guests. All the evening he never left her side, and he whispered a thousand tender things to her as they sat beneath the palms on the terrace.

" You are the lady of my heart," said he. " Why are you so cruel to me that you will not even tell me your name ? "

Cinderella was silent, but she could not help wondering what the Prince would say if he could see her at home, in her dingy kitchen, washing up the greasy crockery, or scrubbing the floor.

So the time passed very pleasantly amid a thousand delights, and Cinderella quite forgot her godmother's warning.

Suddenly she was horrified to hear the big clock in the tower strike the first note of twelve.

With a cry of alarm she sprang to her feet, and without even pausing to say good-bye, rushed out of the ballroom, down the steps of the terrace and into the palace garden. So great was her haste that one of her glass slippers came off and she did not even notice her loss.

Four, five, six ! chimed the clock, and Cinderella ran as she had never run before. She lost herself in the shrubberies, and found her way out again, blundered among the flower-beds, and snapped the roses from their stalks in the speed of her flight.

Seven, eight, nine !

She crossed a lawn and found herself on a wide drive bordered by trees, which she knew must lead to the palace gates.

Ten, eleven, twelve !

And on the stroke of twelve her beautiful gown changed into the ragged dress of a kitchen-maid.

All that remained of her finery was one glass slipper, which she took off and hid carefully away.

A few minutes afterwards the guards at the palace gate saw the figure of a poorly dressed girl flit by. They wondered who she could be, and what she was doing in the grounds at that hour, but the matter seemed very

unimportant, and they had all had a good supper, so
they did not bother to go after her to ask questions.

Cinderella ran all the way home, and arrived at last panting and breathless, just in time to open the door for the sisters.

She asked them whether they had enjoyed themselves as much as on the previous night, and whether the beautiful Princess had been at the ball. They told her all about it, not because they wished to please her—for, as Euphronia said, it was mere waste of time to talk to a kitchen-slut like Cinderella about such fashionable doings —but because they were so excited that they simply had to talk to somebody.

" And what do you think ! " said Charlotte, after her sister had related how the Princess, on the stroke of twelve, had rushed away, leaving her slipper behind. " What do you think ! The Prince kept that slipper in his hand all the rest of the evening, and I saw him kiss it when he thought nobody was looking.

" Foolish creature ! " cried Euphronia with a toss of her head.

" I do not know about that," remarked Charlotte. " It is plain to see that the Prince loves that beautiful lady and will never be happy until he finds her again."

At these words the tears filled Cinderella's eyes, and she had to turn away quickly for fear her sisters should notice her agitation.

" It is the Princess he loves," she thought sadly. " If he could see me now in these ragged clothes, or find me at my drudgery in the kitchen, would he recognize me?

And even if he did know me again, would he not be horrified to think that he had danced with a kitchen-maid ? "

And then she thought that everything was better as it was. The Prince would never see her again, and in time, perhaps, he might forget. But Cinderella would never forget. She knew that all her life long the memory of those two happy evenings would remain with her always, like a beautiful dream.

CHAPTER X

THE GLASS SLIPPER

CHARLOTTE was right. Though the Prince had only spent two evenings in Cinderella's company he already loved her very dearly, not only because of her beauty, but because of her sweet nature, which nobody could help seeing. He felt sure that she must be in some trouble, otherwise she would not have run away from the ball so suddenly, and he made up his mind to find her, and protect her from any one who would do her harm.

The first thing he did was to go into the courtyard, for he thought he might just be in time to see her before her carriage drove away. When he got there, however, he was astonished to hear that the carriage, with all its horses and footmen, had absolutely disappeared. No one had seen the carriage drive away, yet not a sign of it was to be seen.

Very much puzzled, the Prince sent a servant to ask the guards at all the other gates whether they had seen the Princess go out; for he thought she might perhaps have sent her carriage away early, and gone home on foot. But the guards were positive that nobody had passed out of the gates except a shabbily dressed girl, whom they took to be one of the scullery-maids.

Now the Prince was not only a very handsome young man, but he was fairly clever also, and in this case love made him sharp. He thought immediately that this poorly dressed maid seen by the guards might be the lady he sought, who had disguised herself for some reason of her own.

" If she went on foot," he said to himself, " she cannot be very far away, and in that case I can certainly discover her." That night he hardly got a wink of sleep, but in the morning he had thought of a plan.

First of all he gave orders that every lady at the Court must come and try on the slipper which Cinderella had left behind. Not one of them was left out.

92   and then the duchesses,

94   and so on to the plain gentlewomen,

until it was the turn of the servants in the kitchen, but
the slipper would not go on the foot of any of them.

After that the Prince sent out a proclamation that every lady in the town and in the country round about, be she high or low, must try on the glass slipper, and that when he found the lady whom the slipper would fit, he would make her his wife.

There was great excitement when this proclamation
was read in the market-place. People knew that something out of the ordinary was afoot as soon as they saw
the Court courier, with his big curly wig and his trumpeters, and they left whatever they were doing and

crowded round him to listen, and to stare at the glass slipper, which a little blackamoor carried on a velvet cushion.

When he had finished reading, he had hardly time to fold up the parchment and put it in his pocket before there were about a hundred women clamouring to try the slipper on.

" Here's a chance that comes only once in a lifetime," said a stout old lady, plumping herself down in the chair which an attendant had set ready. " One does not get the opportunity of marrying a King's son every day ! " And she waggled her fat foot and tried to work her toes into the dainty shoe which was at least six sizes too small.

Then they all came, one after the other, citizens' and shopkeepers' daughters, and tried their utmost to get the slipper to go on. Many of them had very small, pretty feet, too, but for some mysterious reason the slipper always seemed a little smaller than the very daintiest foot. The truth is, of course, that it was a magic slipper, and could by no means be made to fit anybody except its rightful owner.

So it was all in vain ; and at last the courier, his trumpeters, and his blackamoor left the town and set off to try their fortune in the country houses.

By this time Cinderella's stepsisters had heard the news and were almost beside themselves with excitement.

" Do you hear, Euphronia ? " cried Charlotte, " the Prince has announced that he will marry the lady whom the slipper fits. I'm perfectly certain that it is just my

size, for I took particular note of the lady's shoes when
she was dancing ! "

" Pooh ! What nonsense ! " answered Euphronia
with a scornful smile. " Everybody knows that you take
nines in shoes, and that is two sizes larger than mine.
For my part, I also took careful note of the glass slippers,
and I am positive they were sevens. Besides, they were
slim and elegant shoes, not at all suitable for massive
feet like yours."

Here Euphronia stretched out her own long and bony
foot, clothed in its red stocking, and gazed at it admir-
ingly, while Charlotte sniffed.

Soon afterwards the sound of the trumpet was heard
outside, and a loud knock came to the door. Cinderella
opened it and showed the courier into the drawing-room,
where the sisters were already sitting, dressed in their
best. After she had shown him in she went into the
kitchen again, for she had not received an invitation
to stay.

The courier read the proclamation, and the servant
knelt down to try the slipper on Charlotte's foot, which
was already extended towards him.

" No, no, I should be first," cried Euphronia. " It
is perfectly useless to try the slipper on Charlotte.
Anybody can see with a glance it is much too
small."

" Nothing of the kind ! " snapped Charlotte,
squeezing her toes into the slipper so that she winced
with the pain. " A little humouring is all that is
necessary ! "

And she insisted on trying again and again, until it was evident that she could never succeed in getting the slipper on, even if she tried for years.

"I told you so!" said Euphronia. "Now it is my turn"; and she stretched out her ugly foot so quickly that she nearly knocked the poor attendant over. She, too, struggled and wriggled, but it was all in vain, and at last the courier became very impatient.

"It is no use, madam," said he, "the slipper will not fit either of you. Are there any other ladies in the house?"

"No," snapped Euphronia, "there are not; and I'm certain that I could get the shoe on if you would only let me try just once more. My foot was almost inside when you snatched the slipper away."

"I think you are mistaken, madam," answered the courier politely; "there was a young girl who opened the door for us. Who was she?"

"What, do you mean Cinderslut?" cried Euphronia, with a mighty scornful laugh. "She, you must know, is our kitchen-maid, who does all our dirty work!"

"No matter," answered the courier firmly. "The Prince's orders are not to leave out anybody, whether of high rank or low, so with your leave I will try."

"This is really infamous!" cried Euphronia, with a stamp of her foot, but it was useless to argue, for the courier without wasting any more words walked into the kitchen. Cinderella rose in surprise as he entered, and even in her ragged working dress she looked so lovely that the courier opened his eyes.

" Will you please sit down, madam," said he, " and try this slipper on ? "

" Madam, indeed ! " sniffed Euphronia. " What next, I wonder ! "

But the courier took no notice of her, for at the very first trial the slipper glided on to Cinderella's dainty foot with the greatest ease.

How the sisters stared ! Euphronia's face turned almost green with rage and envy, while Charlotte glared. But their surprise was as nothing to the shock they received the next moment, for Cinderella calmly took the other shoe from her pocket and put it on the other foot. These were the pair of them, gleaming and flashing so that her feet seemed shod with light.

" Well I never ! " muttered Euphronia. " Of all the deceitful little——"

And then she stopped suddenly, for another figure had come into the room—out of nowhere, as it appeared ; for one moment she wasn't there and the next she stood smiling behind Cinderella's chair. It was the figure of an old woman dressed in a red petticoat, with a pointed hat on her head.

She lifted her stick and touched the girl lightly on the shoulder. In that moment Cinderella's rags dropped away, and she appeared dressed in the beautiful gown of white silk in which she had first gone to the ball. She looked so lovely as she sat there that the courier fell on his knees and kissed her hand, as one kisses the hand of a queen.

Then the old godmother spoke, and her voice was very stern and hard.

"Proud and cruel girls," she said, "look upon the sister whom you have despised and have used so spitefully. She is the daughter of the house, but you robbed her of all the joy that should have been hers. Now she shall be the greatest lady in the land, and you shall creep to her feet for forgiveness."

And that is just what the stepsisters did, weeping and

crying for pardon; but Cinderella, whose kind heart
felt pity for their discomfiture, raised them with a kiss.
And this is a thing not many girls would have done who
had suffered as Cinderella had suffered at these girls'
hands, but she had a sweet and gentle nature.

She even kissed the Baroness, who came into the
room just in time to see her daughters kneeling, and who
dropped her lorgnette in surprise.

Then the fairy godmother said that the carriage was

waiting, and they all went down into the courtyard, where they found the magnificent gilt coach, with its six grey horses already harnessed and the coachman and lackeys in their place.

So Cinderella drove away, and there was no happier man in all the world than the Prince when he saw her again, and knew that she would not go away any more. Cinderella, too, was happy, for she loved him and wished for nothing better than to be his wife.

A week later they were married with great pomp and
ceremony. The rejoicings lasted a full week, and all the
town made holiday. Euphronia and Charlotte were at
the wedding and they never uttered a single spiteful
word, not even below their breath, for they were really
sorry for their conduct. As soon as she was settled
down, Cinderella sent for them and gave them each a
suite of grand apartments at the palace. Not long afterwards they married two gentlemen of the Court, and

110   Cinderella and the Prince lived very happily together for the rest of their lives.